THE
MISSING
MARLIN

BALLPARK Mysteries 8

THE MISSING MARLIN

by David A. Kelly

illustrated by Mark Meyers

A STEPPING STONE BOOK™
Random House 🏠 New York

*This book is dedicated to the memory of my grandfather
Charles F. Murnane, an all-around athlete and high school
baseball coach who achieved a 139–32 record in sixteen seasons.
—D.A.K.*

*For Luke, Darrien, Ily, and Mara. Stay nerdy!
—M.M.*

"Hit 'em where they ain't."
*—"Wee Willie" Keeler on the secret of his forty-five-game hitting
streak in 1897*

Text copyright © 2014 by David A. Kelly
Cover art and interior illustrations copyright © 2014 by Mark Meyers

Visit us on the Web!
SteppingStonesBooks.com
randomhouse.com/kids

Educators and librarians, for a variety of teaching tools, visit us at
RHTeachersLibrarians.com

Library of Congress Cataloging-in-Publication Data
Kelly, David A. (David Andrew)
The missing marlin / by David A. Kelly ; illustrated by Mark Meyers. — First edition.
pages cm. — (Ballpark mysteries ; 8)
"A Stepping Stone book."
Summary: "Mike and Kate are visiting the Miami Marlins ballpark when some rare animals from the ballpark's fish tanks go missing." — Provided by publisher.
ISBN 978-0-307-97782-3 (pbk.) — ISBN 978-0-307-97783-0 (lib. bdg.) —
ISBN 978-0-307-97784-7 (ebook)
[1. Fishes—Fiction. 2. Rare animals—Fiction. 3. Miami Marlins (Baseball team)—Fiction. 4. Cousins—Fiction. 5. Miami (Fla.)—Fiction. 6. Mystery and detective stories.]
I. Meyers, Mark, illustrator. II. Title.
PZ7.K2936Mi 2014 [Fic]—dc23 2013008420

Printed in the United States of America
10 9 8 7 6 5 4 3 2 1

Contents

Under the Sea

Mike Walsh puffed out his cheeks and blew with all his might. A stream of seawater shot out of his snorkel. It arched over the deck of Uncle Oliver's boat and hit his cousin Kate Hopkins in the back of the neck.

"Hey!" Kate turned around. "What are you, a fountain? Remember, we're here to see the marlins, not goof around!"

Mike grinned. His freckles stood out even more in the Florida sun. "Do you mean the fish or the baseball team?" he asked.

Kate's mom grabbed a towel from a seat at the back of the boat and handed it to Kate. Kate dried her brown ponytail, which poked out from her baseball cap. "Both! Today we're looking for fish," she said, and pointed to the picture of a blue marlin on her T-shirt. The marlin had a long spear-like nose and a tall fin along the top of its body. "We'll see the *Miami Marlins* tomorrow."

"Well, these are the marlins *I* want to see," Mike said. He tapped the Miami Marlins logo on his shirt. It showed a blue and orange marlin coming out of a big colorful letter *M*.

Mike and Kate were visiting Florida—and their uncle Oliver—with Kate's mom, Laura Hopkins. She was a sports reporter for the American Sportz website. Mrs. Hopkins was writing a story about the Miami Marlins baseball team. That morning Uncle Oliver had driven them from his house in Miami down to the Florida Keys to go snorkeling. He'd promised there'd be lots of colorful fish.

"I have my own favorite Marlin," Uncle Oliver said. He had a bushy mustache and a large belly. "Maybe you'll meet him later." He tied the boat to a mooring anchor bobbing in the water. "The park ranger told me this would be a good place to snorkel. But remember—all the fish and animals in this area are protected, so don't touch any of 'em."

"Or the coral! On the plane, I read that the coral reefs in Florida are in danger," Kate said. She loved to read.

Uncle Oliver nodded. "Yup. Florida's coral reefs stretch from the Dry Tortugas islands in the south all the way up past Miami," he said. "They make a great home for fish."

Uncle Oliver knew a lot about sea life.

He was an animal expert who raised exotic
fish. He ran a nature center called Panther
Park. The workers at Panther Park helped
injured animals and took care of animals
that the police had rescued from poachers
and smugglers.

"The story I read said that poachers steal fish and sometimes coral, too," Kate said.

"What's a poacher?" Mike asked. "Someone who cooks eggs?"

"You're always thinking about food, aren't you?" Kate said. "Poachers aren't cooks. They're people who take animals illegally. Do you think we'll see any, Uncle Oliver?"

"Doubt it," Uncle Oliver said. "But people do pay a lot of money for rare animals and fish. And even coral, I guess. Instead of looking for poachers, you might want to watch for a real marlin. Did you know they can grow to be fourteen feet or longer?"

"Wow!" Kate said.

"They're also fast swimmers," Uncle Oliver said. "They can go over sixty miles per hour!"

"If I see one, I'm going to try to ride it!" Mike said. He pretended to make waves with his hand.

"How about sharks? Are there any around here?"

"Some," Uncle Oliver said. "But I don't think you need to worry 'bout them."

"Well, when I see a shark, I know what to do," Mike said. He made a fist with his right hand and smacked it into his other hand. "I'm going to punch it in the nose! It makes them go away. That's what they said on TV."

Uncle Oliver laughed. "I've heard that, too, but I'm not sure it really works," he said. "When you're done snorkeling, I have something special to share with you in Miami."

"Is it a shark?" Kate asked.

"Not quite," Uncle Oliver said. "But there will be fish. I'm going to the Marlins' ballpark to unveil my new baseball fish. Would you like to come with me?" The Miami Marlins had hired Uncle Oliver to oversee two aquariums in their ballpark. He had bred a special fish for the team that was shaped like a baseball.

"That would be great!" Kate said. "Are you sure it's okay?"

"*No problema, amiga,*" Uncle Oliver said. "As long as Mike doesn't try to punch any of *my* fish!"

Mike laughed. "I won't punch them," he said. Then he pretended to swing a baseball bat. "But since they're baseball fish, I might get confused and try hitting them!"

Kate groaned. "Come on," she said. "Let's go snorkeling!"

Kate, Mike, and Mrs. Hopkins put on their bright yellow snorkels and masks. One end of the snorkel went into their mouths. The other end was made to poke up above the water so they could breathe without lifting their faces. Meanwhile the masks let them see clearly underwater. They all slipped large plastic fins

on their feet. The fins made it easy to swim as they looked for fish.

Uncle Oliver stayed on the boat while Mrs. Hopkins, Mike, and Kate slid from the back into the bright blue sea. The sun reflected off their swim masks until they dropped their heads into the ocean.

For the next half hour, they floated face-down in the calm water, watching the fish under them. Mrs. Hopkins snorkeled near the boat, while Mike and Kate explored. Mike saw silvery fish with yellow tails and lots of little fish that looked almost clear. He watched a school of small fish. He motioned for Kate to follow. The fish darted in and out of the coral reefs. Mike couldn't believe how many fish there were. But it was getting a little hard for him to see them. His mask was starting to fog up. Uncle Oliver had said that might happen.

Kate pointed at a large green turtle swimming past. Mike peered through his foggy goggles and gave her a thumbs-up. He liked the way the turtle moved its front flippers to swim and its back flippers to steer.

Kate was just about to swim over to the boat when she started making wild movements with her arms to get Mike's attention. She motioned for him to turn the other way.

Mike shrugged, kicked his fins, and spun around. He couldn't believe what he saw.

A big black shark was coming straight at him!

Turtle Trouble

Mike clenched his fist to punch the shark. His breathing sped up. If only he could see better!

Suddenly, the shark shot forward.

Mike tightened his fist.

But it swam right past him!

Mike lowered his hand. His breathing returned to normal. If his face hadn't been underwater, he would have laughed.

It wasn't a shark at all!

From far away the black object had looked like a shark through Mike's foggy goggles.

But when it passed by, he could see that it was only a scuba diver in a black wet suit and mask. He held a net, and a black mesh bag trailed along behind him. Kate turned and swam after the scuba diver.

Mike let his feet drop. He popped his head above the water and spit out the snorkel. Finally, Kate swam over. They used their fins to tread water.

"Did you see that?" Mike asked. "That scuba diver looked like a shark!"

"You've just got sharks on the brain," Kate said. "I'm glad you didn't try out your shark punch."

"Why'd you follow him?" Mike asked.

"I thought I saw him trying to catch a fish," Kate said. "That's why he went past you so fast. He was chasing a bright blue fish with his net! But I couldn't keep up with him."

"Too bad," Mike said.

Mike and Kate swam back to the boat. Mrs. Hopkins was already on board. When Uncle Oliver saw them coming, he sounded the horn.

TOOT! TOOT!

"Just in time," Mrs. Hopkins said. She gave Kate and Mike a hand up. "We need to leave for the Marlins' stadium so Uncle Oliver can show everyone his baseball fish!"

Kate and Mike grabbed towels and dried off. They sank onto the seats as Uncle Oliver drove the boat back to the dock.

Kate spent most of the hour-long car ride studying one of Uncle Oliver's books on endangered animals. She tried to show Mike some of the pictures, but he was more interested in bouncing his tennis ball off the side window. He always carried a ball with him.

Back in Miami, they headed straight to

the stadium. After a security guard in a blue suit waved them through the employees' door, Uncle Oliver led them to the infield. A group of reporters with cameras mingled around home plate.

Kate had never seen a ballpark with so many colors. The hallways were bright shades of green, red, yellow, and blue. The outfield fence and wall were lime green. A huge set of windows behind the outfield faced downtown Miami.

"This stadium sure doesn't feel like most baseball stadiums," Mrs. Hopkins said. "It's so colorful!"

"Awesome!" Mike said. "What's that?" He pointed at a huge sculpture just behind the center-field wall. The sculpture looked like an island with large pink flamingos, palm trees, the sun and ocean, and, of course, marlins.

"It's the Marlins' home run sculpture," Uncle Oliver said. "When a Marlin hits a home run, the fish jump, the birds fly, and jets of water shoot up!"

Kate looked in the other direction, toward home plate. "Look—a fish tank!" she said. On

the left side of home plate was a twenty-two-foot-long clear tank filled with coral. It was built into the infield wall, right in front of the first row of seats. All types of small fish swam in it.

"Where's the second tank?" Mike asked. "I thought there were two."

Uncle Oliver pointed to the other side of the plate, near the third-base line. A long white cloth covered part of the infield wall. "It's under that drape," he said. "That's where my rare baseball fish are."

Kate couldn't take her eyes off the beautiful blue water. Mike seemed more interested in looking at the edges of the tank.

"Boy, this glass must be really thick," he said. "What if a ball hits it?"

Uncle Oliver twirled the end of his mustache. "No problem," he said. "The Marlins put super-strong glass in front of the tanks. They even had a Marlins pitcher fire balls at it to make sure it wouldn't break."

"Wow, that would be the perfect job for you," Kate said to Mike. "You're great at breaking windows with baseballs."

Mike rolled his eyes. Kate was right, but he

didn't like to admit it. "Well, that means I have lots of power!" he said.

"The only power you have is the power to make accidents happen." Kate laughed.

Uncle Oliver cleared his throat. "Will you two excuse me?" he asked. "It looks like things are starting. I'll see you back at my house tonight after dinner. I have a meeting with my banker later."

Kate and Mike nodded. Uncle Oliver ambled over to the other side of the infield.

"And I have to go interview the team president," Mrs. Hopkins said. "I'll catch you afterward." She dug a notebook out of her bag and headed for home plate.

"Hey, there's Guppy Gomez," Mike said. "He's the Marlins' best pitcher. I'm going to see if he'll teach me something."

Guppy was standing near the pitching

mound. He was tall and thin with big feet and hands. Mike waited for him to finish talking to a reporter. Then Mike asked him a question. Kate watched as Guppy leaned down, gave Mike a baseball, and showed him how to hold it. Fifteen minutes later, Mike came running back.

"That was great!" Mike said with a wide smile. "Guppy showed me how to throw gyroballs, forkballs, and even an Eephus pitch!"

"What's an Eephus pitch?" Kate asked.

"It's when a pitcher throws the ball super slow and high," Mike said. "Like twenty feet up. It arcs and falls over the plate. It's really hard to hit."

A tapping sound came from home plate. Buck Thompson, the Marlins team president, stepped up to a microphone on a stand. "I'd like to welcome everyone here to the unveiling of a very unusual addition to the Marlins' stadium," he said. "It's a set of rare baseball fish raised by Oliver O'Brien, our friend from Panther Park."

An assistant pulled the white cover off the

fish tank. The crowd of reporters took pictures. Camera flashes blinked one after another.

The second fish tank looked just like the first. But in the middle swam two white fish with red splotches.

"Why did you name them baseball fish?" a reporter called out.

Uncle Oliver leaned forward. "You'll see shortly," he said. "Just keep an eye on them."

Mike, Kate, and the crowd of reporters watched the red-and-white fish. Nothing happened for a few minutes. Some of the reporters started shifting around and talking.

"Look!" one cried out. A hush fell over the reporters. Inside the tank, the two fish stared out at the crowd. But they had both puffed out their bodies like balloons. The splotches of red scales now looked completely different. They looked like the red stitching on a baseball!

"Hey, they're like two swimming baseballs!" one man said.

The other reporters and Uncle Oliver laughed. "You're right," he said. "Now you know why we call them baseball fish."

The reporters took more pictures. Some talked with Uncle Oliver. Mrs. Hopkins stood off to the side, interviewing one of the Marlins. Mike and Kate came close for a better look at the baseball fish. "They're cool," Kate said. "I've never seen anything like them!"

After a while, Mike and Kate wandered back to the fish tank on the first-base side, where it was quieter. Kate studied the fish while Mike tossed his baseball up in the air and caught it.

Finally, Mrs. Hopkins finished her interview. She signaled for the kids to follow her up the stairs to the exit. Most of the other reporters

had left. Uncle Oliver was nowhere to be seen.

Mike scrambled after Mrs. Hopkins. At the top of the stairs, he turned to check on Kate. But she wasn't behind him. Mike scanned the infield. At last he spotted Kate in front of the tank. She hadn't moved at all!

"Kate!" Mike called. He pointed at a pretend watch on his wrist. "Time to go!"

Kate shook her head and looked at the tank closely one more time. Then she started running up the steps. Mike turned to follow Mrs. Hopkins.

By the time Kate caught up to Mike, she was panting.

"You'll never believe what I just saw down there," she said.

"What?" Mike asked.

"There's an endangered sea turtle in the Marlins' fish tank!"

Panther Patrol

Back at Uncle Oliver's house, Kate sat down in front of her mother's laptop computer. She pulled up a page filled with photos of green sea turtles. They had long necks and shiny eyes.

"That's what I saw in the Marlins' tank!" Kate said. "What was it doing there, Ned?"

Ned was Uncle Oliver's assistant at Panther Park. Uncle Oliver was still at his meeting, but Ned had just come in from feeding the animals. He wore a maroon shirt, tan shorts, and hiking boots. Ned leaned over and took a closer look at the screen. Then he scratched his chin.

"Those are endangered green sea turtles, all right," Ned said. "But there are no turtles in the Marlins' tank. Your uncle and I keep tight control over what goes in there. One of us checks the tanks before each and every game."

Kate crossed her arms. "I definitely saw one in the tank!" she said.

Mrs. Hopkins looked at the turtles. "Maybe it was just a piece of coral or something," she said. "I don't think the Marlins would keep endangered species in their tanks at the ballpark."

"You sure you're not seeing things?" Mike asked.

Kate glared at Mike. She reached out to pinch him, but he jumped away. "Don't you believe me?" she asked.

Ned stepped forward. "I'm sure you *think* you saw one," he said. "Why don't you ask your uncle to inspect the tanks with you before tomorrow's game?"

"I guess," Kate said. She made a face at Mike. "Then I'll be able to *prove* I was right!"

Ned opened the door. "I've got to check on a few more animals," he said. "I'll see you later."

After Ned left, Mike and Mrs. Hopkins played a game of checkers, and Kate read more about endangered animals. In a little while, Uncle Oliver came back. He walked in, dropped his briefcase on the table, and gave a deep sigh.

"What's the matter?" Mrs. Hopkins asked.

"I'm okay, but Panther Park isn't," he said. "I've just had a meeting about it. We barely have enough money to stay open. It's costing too much to feed and take care of all the animals rescued from poachers and smugglers.

The money we get from visitors isn't enough."

"Oh no!" Kate said. "If you close, what will happen to the animals?"

"If we have to shut down, we'll try to get them good homes at other zoos and aquariums," Uncle Oliver said.

"Well, I know where one endangered animal found a home!" Kate said. She told Uncle Oliver about the rare turtle she'd seen at the ballpark.

Uncle Oliver listened to Kate, then shook his head. "I don't think we have a turtle in our tank," he said. "But I can bring you in early to have a look, just in case."

Uncle Oliver checked his watch. It was just after seven-thirty. "Would you like a tour of Panther Park?"

Kate brightened up. "Sure," she said.

Uncle Oliver led Mike, Kate, and Mrs. Hopkins out the back door of the house onto

a big wooden deck. Even though it was after dinner, the sun was still up. They followed a wooden boardwalk past towering trees and lots of green plants. The air felt warm and moist and hummed with the sound of crickets and other insects.

The path led into a sandy area with large habitats on either side. Mike and Kate ran over to the one on the right. Two large cats with yellow eyes prowled along the fences at the edges of their habitat. Their fur was a deep tan color, but their ears and the ends of their tails were black.

"You might know those cats as cougars, pumas, or mountain lions," Uncle Oliver said. "But down here we call them Florida panthers. In fact, they're our state animal. We rescued these from a poacher who was selling them."

"They're beautiful!" Kate said. She took

pictures of the panthers. Then she noticed a sign in front of the habitat. It stated that panthers don't roar. Instead, they growl, hiss, whistle, and purr. The sign also noted they can weigh up to 130 pounds or more.

"What's that?" Mike asked. He ran over to a wooden pen on the other side of the clearing. "Cool! An armadillo! Kate, come see."

The armadillo looked like a little pig with a hard shell on its back. It had a narrow head with small ears and a long tail covered with a leathery shell. Kate snapped some pictures of it.

"Most people think you only find armadillos in Texas," Uncle Oliver said. "But Florida has them, too. I guess they like our weather. This one is recovering from an injury."

"Hey, look!" Kate said. She pointed at the sign in front of the pen. "*Armadillo* means *little armored one* in Spanish." Kate was interested in anything that had to do with Spanish. Her father had learned to speak Spanish because he was a baseball scout and he worked with lots of players who spoke the language. Kate's father often wrote her emails in Spanish so Kate could learn, too.

"All that armor looks a little uncomfortable to me," Mike said. "I'd rather just wear a T-shirt!"

Uncle Oliver laughed. "I don't think I'd like a hard shell on me, either, especially since it gets so hot around here," he said. He waved his hand. "Come on. I've got something else to show you."

Uncle Oliver led them down a path between tall coconut palm trees. High overhead the long leaves rustled in the evening breeze. The path ended near a small, brightly colored building.

Uncle Oliver gave a sharp whistle. A moment later, the door opened and Ned stepped out.

But he wasn't alone. He had two large parrots on his shoulders. One was mostly green with bright blue feathers. The other had red head feathers and green and blue tail feathers.

Ned placed the green-and-blue parrot on Mike's shoulder. After standing for a moment, the parrot started strutting back and forth.

"Hey, that tickles!" Mike said as he tried to hold still. But the parrot ignored Mike's wiggles. It seemed very happy on his shoulder.

"You look like a pirate!" Kate said. "Ahoy, matey!"

"Let's make you look like a pirate, too," Ned said to Kate. He had her stick her right arm out in front of her. He placed the red-and-green parrot on her wrist.

"Oh wow!" Kate said. "This is great! I thought its claws would hurt, but I can barely feel them!"

Mrs. Hopkins took pictures of Kate and Mike with their birds. Then the red-and-green one hopped onto Mike's wrist. Mike put the green-and-blue one on Kate's shoulder. Finally, Ned took the birds back to their roost.

"I've saved the best for last," Uncle Oliver said. "Let me show you where we raise my baseball fish. You can also get a peek at my favorite one of all. He has the brightest red markings yet. I've named him Marlin, after the team."

Uncle Oliver led them through the clearing to a large black-and-white building. Once they were through the doorway, Uncle Oliver flipped on the lights. The room was filled with fish tanks.

Uncle Oliver gasped.

"What's the matter?" Mrs. Hopkins asked. "Is anything wrong?"

Uncle Oliver reached out his hand to the wall to steady himself.

"Yes," he said. "Marlin is missing!"

Fish and
Gummy Sharks

The next day, Kate and Mike quietly opened the door to the baseball fish building.

"You sure it's okay to be here?" Mike whispered to Kate.

"Yes." Kate nodded. "Uncle Oliver *said* we could look around."

"But I'm not sure he wanted us going inside the buildings!" Mike said. He bounced his green tennis ball on the concrete floor.

It was Friday morning. Mrs. Hopkins was

back at the house, working on her story. Uncle Oliver had told Mike and Kate they could explore the nature center grounds if they wanted. Later that morning they were heading to the Marlins' ballpark for a game.

"Come on," Kate said. "We only have an hour until Panther Park opens. We need to look for clues to help Uncle Oliver. I'll start near the windows. You check by the fish tanks. You know what we're looking for?"

"Anything *fishy*," Mike said with a smile. "Get it? *Fish* tanks. Fishy . . ."

Kate rolled her eyes at Mike's bad pun. "Look for anything strange," she said. She bent down to look at the window frame. "If Uncle Oliver won't go to the police, we're his only chance."

After they had discovered the night before that Uncle Oliver's favorite fish, Marlin, was missing, their uncle had told them a secret. It wasn't the first time someone had stolen his fish. Two baseball fish had been taken the week before. But Uncle Oliver didn't want to call the police. He was worried the Marlins might fire him from taking care of their fish tanks and hire someone else. And without the Marlins job, Uncle Oliver wouldn't have enough money to keep Panther Park open.

"First we have an endangered turtle. Now we have missing fish," Kate said while she was searching. "Those are two strange things. I think they're connected."

"I don't know, Kate," Mike said. "It may only be missing fish. Nobody else has seen your phantom turtle!"

"You'll see it later this morning when we check the tanks with Uncle Oliver," Kate said. "It'll prove I was right."

Mike and Kate searched the fish tank room

for twenty minutes but didn't find any clues.
Kate was about to give up when Mike stopped
her. He pointed to a small crack between the
fish tanks and a heavy desk.

"I think I see something in there," he said. "Help me move the desk."

Mike and Kate pulled the desk a few inches to the right. As they did, something dropped to the ground.

Mike picked up an inch-long object. It was bright blue and shaped like a shark. It even had a little blue fin on its back.

"Know what this is?" he asked.

"I sure do," Kate said. "But just because you eat them all the time! It's a gummy shark."

"Exactly," Mike said. "I think it's a clue. Maybe the thief dropped it while he was taking the baseball fish."

"Or *she*," Kate said. "We don't know if the thief is a man or woman. Or if some kid stuck it in here."

"Nah, I know it's a clue," Mike said.

Just then, Mike heard a noise outside the

building. Mike and Kate glanced at each other. But before they could move, Ned stepped through the doorway.

"What are you two doing here?" Ned asked. "The nature center isn't open yet!"

"Uncle Oliver said we could look around. We're searching for clues to the missing fish. Look what we found!" Mike said. He held out the gummy shark. "We think the thief dropped this by mistake!"

Ned's eyebrows went up. He looked at the candy for a moment. Then he smiled. "I'm not sure that will help you much," he said. "Kids drop all sorts of stuff. Especially candy, which they're not supposed to eat in here."

"Shoot," Mike said. "I thought it was a real clue."

"Good try, though," Ned said. "I'll let you know if I find anything while I'm working."

"Thanks!" Kate said. "We'll see you later."

They weren't leaving for the game for another hour, so Mike and Kate went back to Uncle Oliver's house. Kate plopped down at Uncle Oliver's desk. She started to poke through one of his many books about animals. Mike sat on the couch. He turned on a sports show on TV.

Kate was just closing the book when she gave a low whistle. "Ah, Mike?" she said. "Can you come here for a minute?"

Mike popped up from the couch. "Why?" he asked. "Did you find a rare turtle hiding in the desk?"

Kate shook her head. She handed him a letter. "This was under the book I was reading," she said. "I wasn't trying to snoop, but the word *insurance* caught my eye."

Mike read the letter. It was from an in-

surance company. It showed that Uncle Oliver had bought a big insurance policy for his baseball fish.

"I hope that doesn't mean what I think it means," Mike said.

"What?" Kate asked. "That Uncle Oliver is smart because he insures his business?"

"There may be more to it," Mike said. He pointed at the bottom line. "Those fish are insured for *a lot* of money."

"So?" Kate replied. "He's just being careful."

"He's being careful not to tell the police!" Mike said. "The more fish that are missing, the more money he'll make."

"What do you mean?" Kate asked.

Mike leaned over. "I hate to say something bad about Uncle Oliver," he whispered. "But what if he's stealing the fish himself for the insurance money?"

Critters and Creatures

"That's crazy!" Kate said.

Mike started pacing back and forth. "I know. But think about it," he said. He ticked off the reasons on his fingers. "Uncle Oliver took out a lot of insurance on the fish. He doesn't want to call the police. He could be in danger of losing his job with the Marlins. And Panther Park is having money troubles. It all fits together."

Kate sank into the chair. She shook her

head. "I don't know," she said. "I really don't think Uncle Oliver is stealing his own fish."

"Well, we have to consider everything," Mike said. "*Someone* is taking the fish!"

"Okay." Kate sighed. "Let's keep an eye on him at the game."

When they arrived at the stadium later that morning, Mrs. Hopkins headed to the pressroom. Uncle Oliver led Mike and Kate to the fish tanks behind home plate to check for Kate's turtle. Kate watched their uncle carefully for any clues.

The stadium was empty except for workers preparing for the day's game. Batting practice wouldn't start for another hour.

"You said you saw the turtle in that tank, right?" Uncle Oliver pointed to the tank along the first-base line. Kate nodded. The three of them scanned the water from top to bottom

and left to right. They saw lots of fish and bright coral. But no turtle.

Kate poked the glass in the middle of the tank. "It was right there," she said. "I definitely saw a small green sea turtle *right there*. It was a little bigger than my hand. Where'd it go?"

Uncle Oliver unlocked the long green top of the tank with a key. He scanned the water from the top. Still, they saw nothing except fish.

Uncle Oliver shut and locked the top. "I know you think you saw a turtle, Kate," he said. "But there's no turtle in there now."

Kate scuffed at the red clay of the warning track with her sneaker. She hated to be wrong.

Just then, a voice called to Uncle Oliver from the stands. A man wearing a Marlins warm-up jacket and a tall man wearing a bright green shirt came down to the infield.

Uncle Oliver shook hands with the man in the Marlins jacket. "Mike and Kate, this is Buck Thompson, the Marlins team president," he said.

Mike and Kate said hello to Buck. Then the man in the green shirt stepped forward. He slapped Uncle Oliver playfully on the back.

"Look what the cat dragged in," he said. He gave Uncle Oliver's shoulder a tight squeeze.

Uncle Oliver winced. He cleared his throat.

"And this is Don Dixon," Uncle Oliver said. "He runs Critters and Creatures, the biggest fish and pet store in town. I think he's a bit jealous that the Marlins hired me to raise their fish!"

Don Dixon snorted. "Oh, don't get ahead of yourself," he said. "They hired you, but they can also fire you! After all, Critters and Creatures is the best fish and pet store in Miami."

"And what does that mean?" Uncle Oliver asked.

Don Dixon waved his hand. "Well, we don't have a nature center to run, so we can focus on the fish," he said. "Anyway, I'm just here for the game. Let's not talk shop."

"Good idea," Uncle Oliver said. "I have to leave for a business meeting soon anyway." He said goodbye to Buck and Don Dixon. Then he nodded at Mike and Kate. "I'll see you two back at the house later. Ned will be by soon to check the tanks before the game. You can help if you want."

As Uncle Oliver headed for the exit, Mike and Kate slipped into a couple of seats right behind the fish tanks to wait for Ned.

Kate stared at Don Dixon. "I don't trust him," she said. "Did you hear how he talked to Uncle Oliver?"

Mike nodded. "He was kinda mean."

Don Dixon and the Marlins president continued their talk near home plate. After a few minutes, Mike nudged Kate. He pointed at Don Dixon. "Look, they're leaving together," he said. "Let's follow them!"

"What about waiting for Ned?" Kate asked.

"We already checked the tanks with Uncle

Oliver," Mike said. "We're not going to miss anything with Ned. I think we need to figure out what Don Dixon is up to!"

Don Dixon and the Marlins president left the infield and walked up the aisle. As they did, Mike and Kate followed. They pretended to play catch with Mike's tennis ball. When the two men reached the top of the steps, they leaned against a railing overlooking the ballpark.

Mike motioned for Kate to throw the ball high. The ball sailed over Mike's head and bounced into the seats just below the two men. Mike scrambled over the seats to get the ball.

"Hey, Kate," he called. "I can't find the ball. Help me out."

When Kate came over, Mike showed her the tennis ball in his hand. But he put his finger to his lips. Above them, behind the railing, Don Dixon and the Marlins president were talking.

Mike and Kate pretended to keep looking for the ball.

The first thing they heard was Don Dixon laughing.

"I know that Oliver's nature center is having some trouble lately," Don Dixon said. "Who knows how much longer he'll be able to keep it going."

Kate's fingers curled into a fist.

"Well, you know we like Oliver a lot. But let me give you a key to the tanks," Buck said. "It might come in handy for what we talked about."

"Thanks," Don Dixon said. "Critters and Creatures would be happy to take over if Oliver runs into problems!"

Guppy Goes Fishing

"See? It's not Uncle Oliver! It's Don Dixon!" Kate said as they found their seats a few minutes later. "He must be trying to cause problems for Uncle Oliver so he can get the Marlins' business! *He's* the one stealing the fish!"

They were sitting about ten rows behind home plate. A group of schoolchildren in bright purple T-shirts was next to them. All around them, the stadium was filling up.

"Maybe," Mike said. "But Uncle Oliver is still a suspect because of that insurance."

"Well, I think it's Don Dixon," Kate said. "We can look for clues at his pet shop. My mom can take us tomorrow."

When the game started, Guppy Gomez ran out to the mound. The other Marlins players jogged out to their positions. The fans cheered. The first batter for the Arizona Diamondbacks took practice swings in the warm-up area.

"This is going to be great," Mike said. "I can't wait to see Guppy pitch."

"Why do they call him Guppy?" Kate asked.

"His name is really Gary Gomez. But they call him Guppy because he gets batters to 'go fishing,'" Mike said. "That means he throws a lot of pitches just outside the strike zone. It looks like a strike so batters swing. But usually they miss or just hit little bloopers for outs."

On the mound, Guppy was ready to pitch. He waited for the sign from the catcher. Then

he twirled the ball in his glove to get it to the right position. He wound up and fired.

The ball sailed toward home plate. But just before the plate, it dropped low and outside. The Diamondbacks batter swung anyway.

"STRIKE ONE!" the umpire called.

The catcher threw the baseball back to the pitcher. Guppy pitched again. This time the ball sailed in higher. But it was still outside the strike zone. The batter swung and missed again.

"STRIKE TWO!" the umpire called.

Mike nudged Kate. "See?" he said. "He's a master at throwing pitches that batters think they can hit but can't!"

Guppy's third pitch was so slow, it bounced on home plate. This time, the batter didn't swing.

"BALL ONE!" the umpire called.

Guppy's fourth pitch was perfect. He threw

a fastball straight down the center. But the batter was too slow on his swing.

"STRIKE THREE!" the umpire called.

Guppy had his first out. It looked like it was going to be a good day for the Marlins.

The next two batters went down just as quickly. Then it was the Marlins' turn to bat. Their first batter led off with a single. The second batter grounded out. But the third hit a double, scoring the man on first. The next two batters struck out. At the end of the first inning, Miami was ahead, 1–0.

Late fans looked for their seats as the Marlins took the field for the second inning. Kate was watching the fans walking by when she noticed something.

"Hey, Mike!" Kate said. "Look over there." She pointed off to their right. "It's Ned."

Ned was sitting in the first row, behind the

first-base fish tank. He seemed to be arguing with the two men dressed in suits next to him.

"Uncle Oliver mentioned that Ned comes to a lot of games," Mike said. "I guess he gets good seats. But you know what I want to get?"

"What?" asked Kate.

"Some good *food*," Mike said. "I'm hungry. I want one of those Cuban sandwiches I've heard about."

"¡Que suena bien!" Kate said. "That sounds good!"

They got up from their seats and wandered toward the Taste of Miami food area near left field. After waiting in line, they ordered two Cuban sandwiches. The man behind the counter layered slices of bread with ham, pork, cheese, and pickles. Then he added some mustard and flattened the sandwich with a heavy press that melted the cheese.

"So *this* is a Cuban sandwich," Mike said after he took a bite. "It's great!"

Kate nodded. She was too busy eating to reply.

"And these plantain chips aren't bad, either," Mike said. He popped another handful into his mouth. "I think I like Miami food!"

After eating, Mike and Kate went back to their seats. Along the way, Mike stopped at a souvenir stand to buy a Marlins baseball and a black marker. "I'm going to see if I can get Guppy's autograph after the game!" he said.

By the time they sat down, the Diamond-backs had tied the score, 1–1. But three innings later, Miami got two more runs. At the bottom of the seventh inning, the Marlins were still ahead, 3–1. They had one man on base and their best hitter, Felix Charles, was up.

Charles didn't hold back. On the second

pitch, the Miami batter popped the ball high into the air. The ball sailed over the infield and headed for the right field wall. It was going, going . . . gone! A home run!

Behind center field, the home run statue Mike had spotted the day before began to move. Large cutouts of marlin fish twirled and circled the statue. Jets of water shot up from the side. Neon lights blinked. Pink flamingos danced. The Marlins' fans cheered.

"Wow, cool!" Mike said.

"I like the flamingos," Kate said.

When the home run statue stopped moving, the game continued. The Marlins didn't score again that inning.

Kate nudged Mike. "Take a look at Ned," she said. "I've been watching him for a while. He's arguing with those two men again. They keep pointing at the fish tank."

Mike looked over. Kate was right. Ned and his friends were staring at the fish tank and jabbering about something.

"That's weird," Mike said. "I've got an idea. Wait here." He stood up and walked down the aisle to an open seat in the third row. A few minutes later, he returned.

"So what are they talking about?" Kate asked.

Mike shook his head. "I don't know," he said.

"They were speaking Spanish. Maybe you can figure it out."

Kate's eyes lit up. She loved to practice her Spanish. She slipped into the same seat that Mike had just been in. Mike pretended to watch the game until Kate came back.

"Did you figure it out?" Mike asked.

Kate nodded. "Yup, I got some of it," she said. "They were talking about the Tortugas. Uncle Oliver mentioned those islands when he was telling us about coral reefs. They said something about money, like they were arguing over an amount."

"What do you think it meant?" Mike asked.

Kate shrugged. "I don't know," she said. "It sounded like they were planning a trip or something."

Mike was disappointed it wasn't more interesting. He settled back into his seat to watch

the rest of the game. Kate kept her eyes on Ned in between plays. The Marlins were still ahead with only one inning left.

Suddenly, Kate nudged Mike. "Look!" she said to him. "Over there!" She pointed to the other side of home plate, near the third-base line. Don Dixon from Critters and Creatures was sitting a few rows behind the infield wall.

"So? We already knew Don Dixon was here," Mike said. "What's the big deal?"

"Look at what he's eating," Kate said.

Mike spotted something yellow in Don Dixon's left hand. It looked like a package of candy. Mike watched as Don tilted it into his other hand. Three bright blue gummy sharks dropped into his palm!

Tortugas

"Think about it, Mike. Don Dixon has a lot to gain if Uncle Oliver runs into problems!" Kate said.

Mike nodded. "Sure, but lots of people eat gummy candy. It doesn't mean he's the thief. And I hate to say it, but the clues against Uncle Oliver are worse."

Out on the field, the Marlins had finished the game, 6–3. Fans started getting up. Mike and Kate watched as Ned and the two men with him left.

"Hang on for a minute, cuz," Mike said. He took the black marker out of his pocket and held up his baseball. "I want to see if I can get some autographs. I'll meet you back here in a minute."

Mike ran down to the infield wall. A small group of kids stood near the dugout, trying to get the players' attention. Mike joined in. He waved his baseball in the air.

While Mike was busy, Kate dropped into one of the front-row seats to watch the fish swim. She noticed two baseball fish in the tank. She waited for them to puff up, but neither did. Then the fish on the left caught her eye. It was brighter than the other one. Kate remembered Uncle Oliver saying that Marlin, one of the missing fish, had bright red markings. Kate shook her head. It was probably just the light.

By the dugout, Mike was having better

luck. The Marlins first baseman had already signed his hat. Now Mike was trying to get Guppy to sign his baseball. Mike held it high so the pitcher would see it.

Guppy was only one person away when Mike felt a tug on his T-shirt.

"Mike! Quick! Come here," Kate said. "You'll never believe what I just found!" She gave his shirt another tug and ran over to the tank.

Mike turned to see Guppy take a step back and wave to the crowd. He wasn't going to sign any more autographs.

"Drat!" Mike said. He had missed his chance. He took one more look at Guppy walking back to the dugout, and then he scrambled after Kate.

Kate stood in front of the fish tank on the first-base side. "Look at this!" she said. "What do you see?"

Mike studied the tank. It looked just like it had before the game. He shrugged. "Um . . . water. Is that a trick question?"

Kate stamped her sneaker on the cement walkway. "No, you sponge head!" she said. "Don't you see what's *in* the water?"

Mike leaned over to look more closely. As he did, a green turtle about ten inches long swam by! A minute later, a second turtle swam past.

"Those are just like the one I saw yesterday!" Kate said. "See? I wasn't imagining things. They're the endangered sea turtles that I saw in Uncle Oliver's book! And look, there are two baseball fish in there! The one on the left has bright red markings, just like Uncle Oliver's missing fish Marlin. I bet that's what Ned and his friends were pointing at during the game!"

"But the turtles weren't there when we checked the tanks with Uncle Oliver," Mike said. "And neither were the baseball fish!"

"I know!" Kate said. "That's because someone put them in the tank after we checked it."

"Maybe it *was* Don Dixon," Mike said. "He

said he'd be happy to take over the tanks from Uncle Oliver. And we know he has a key to the tanks."

Kate nodded. "Maybe," she said. "But it could be someone else."

"What do you mean?" Mike asked.

"It could be Ned! Remember when I overheard Ned and those men speaking Spanish during the game?" Kate asked. "I thought they were talking about the Tortugas islands that Uncle Oliver had mentioned when he told us about coral reefs. But maybe they weren't!"

Mike looked puzzled. "What were they talking about, then?" he asked.

Kate pointed at the two turtles. "When I saw these, I remembered something. *Tortuga* means *turtle* in Spanish!" she said. "They might have been talking about these turtles. Not the islands."

"Oh wow!" Mike said. "But weren't they talking about taking a trip to the islands?"

"They were talking about money, but maybe they weren't talking about a trip," Kate said. "Maybe they were deciding how much to pay for the turtles!"

"Whoa! So you think Ned's selling rare turtles?" Mike asked.

"And fish! Ned could be the connection between Uncle Oliver's missing fish and these turtles," Kate said. "He must be taking the fish from Panther Park!"

"What happened to the turtle you saw yesterday?" Mike asked. "Why wasn't it here this morning?"

"Because Ned sold it!" Kate said. "He sells the fish in this tank and replaces them with new ones from Uncle Oliver's place. Maybe he's working with Don Dixon and the pet store. But I don't know where Ned got the turtles."

Mike snapped his fingers. "I know! How about where we went snorkeling yesterday?" he asked. "Maybe Ned or Don Dixon was the scuba-diving shark that I saw! The mesh bag was for the turtles!"

Kate nodded. "So if Ned's the thief, he must put new fish in before games and take them out after," she said. "If that's it, then those men next to him weren't planning a trip. They were bidding on exotic fish and endangered turtles!"

A Cooler Getaway

"Do you see anything?" Mike whispered.

Kate shook her head. "No sign of anyone yet," she said.

Mike and Kate were huddled behind the infield wall. By now, almost all the fans had left the stadium. The grounds crew was busy getting the infield ready for the next day's game. From their hiding spot, Mike and Kate could keep a direct eye on the tank with the turtles and the baseball fish.

Kate checked the time. "My mom said she'd

give us thirty minutes. She's still working on her story."

They crouched quietly for ten minutes. But no one came close.

"Think this will work?" Mike asked.

"We know that *someone's* putting turtles in the tanks and taking them out," Kate said. "So *someone* must be coming by after the game. It's either going to be Don Dixon or Ned."

"Or Uncle Oliver," Mike said sadly.

Kate glared at him. "It's not our uncle," she said.

After ten more minutes, Mike's knees began to ache. "How about if I just sit over there and you call me if anything happens?" he asked.

"No, we both need to watch," Kate said. "And if the thief sees you in the seats, he may not pick up the fish and turtles!"

The minutes ticked by. The stadium was

completely empty except for the cleaning crew.

Kate checked the time again and sighed. They were supposed to meet her mother in five minutes.

Mike dropped to the ground. "Let's just go," he said. "This isn't going to work."

Kate ignored him. A minute later, she gasped and pointed to the field. Mike popped his head around the corner and looked.

Uncle Oliver was walking down the aisle toward the tanks!

"Oh no!" Mike said. "It's Uncle Oliver!"

"I can't believe Uncle Oliver is stealing his own fish!" Kate slumped against the side of the wall. "I guess he's working with Ned to sell them. That way, he'll get the insurance money."

Mike nodded. "Geez, Kate, I think you're right. Take a look at this," he said.

Kate peeked around the edge of the wall.

Uncle Oliver had stopped to talk to someone. It was Ned! Kate shook her head and frowned.

Uncle Oliver turned and walked back up the stairs to the exit. Meanwhile, Ned looked around nervously. He took a step toward the fish tank near Kate and Mike.

As Ned got closer, they saw he was carrying two black coolers.

Mike and Kate watched Ned open the top of the tank. He checked to see if anyone was watching him. When he decided no one was, he quickly dipped a net into the tank and pulled out a turtle. He slipped the turtle into one of the coolers. Ned did the same thing with the other turtle and the two baseball fish.

All the while, Kate snapped pictures with her camera. "Now we have proof that Ned's taking the fish!" she whispered.

When he was finished, Ned put the top

back on the tank. He picked up the coolers and headed for the exit.

Kate put the camera into her pocket. "We've got to stop him," she said.

Mike and Kate scrambled through the seats to the aisle. But it was blocked by a cleaning crew sweeping up. By the time they made it to the top of the stairs, Ned had reached the ballpark exit. He opened the door and left.

"Drat! We've lost him!" Kate said.

"No, we haven't," Mike said. "Come on. Pretend you just hit a triple and run as fast as you can!" Mike took off running. Kate followed. Their sneakers slapped against the concrete floor.

Mike reached the exit door first. He pushed it open. Ned was right ahead of them. He stood on the corner, waiting to cross the street.

"We've got him!" Mike said. They sprinted

to the corner. The light turned, and Ned started across.

But just as Ned stepped off the sidewalk, Mike grabbed the cooler on the right. Kate took the one on the left. They wrenched the coolers out of his hands.

Ned spun around. "What are you doing?" he asked. "Don't fool around with those. I'm delivering fish."

Mike and Kate stood their ground. "Yeah," Mike said. "You're delivering *stolen* fish and endangered turtles!"

Ned shook his head and laughed. "You're crazy," he said. "I've just been doing a test of the filters. I'm returning the fish to their own tanks."

Ned took a step toward Kate's cooler.

"Not so fast," Kate said. She moved the cooler closer to Mike.

Ned looked like he was about to push Kate and Mike aside. But a voice called out from behind them.

"Need help?"

Mike and Kate turned around. It was Don Dixon!

"Oh no!" Kate said.

"Rats!" Mike said. "Don Dixon's going to help Ned escape!"

A Big Catch

Kate's shoulders sank as Don Dixon ran over. There was no way she and Mike could stop both Don and Ned. The men were going to escape with the stolen animals!

Thinking quickly, Mike pushed the two black coolers behind them. But instead of trying to snatch them, Don Dixon reached out and grabbed Ned!

"Got him!" he said. "Thanks to you two!" Don Dixon held Ned by his arm. He dragged him back toward the Marlins' stadium. "I just called security. They should be here shortly."

Mike and Kate exchanged glances. What was going on? They picked up the coolers and followed Don Dixon back to the stadium.

Just as Don reached the main entrance, a security car pulled up. The officer jumped out and handcuffed Ned.

Don Dixon walked over to Mike and Kate. "I think they can take it from here," he said. "Thanks for stopping Ned before he got away."

"But we thought you were helping Ned steal the animals!" Kate said. "You told Buck that you'd love to manage the fish tanks!"

Don Dixon laughed. "I can see why you'd think that," he said. "I was only teasing your uncle about the tanks. I wouldn't want to take the business away from him. Buck just asked me to keep an eye on the tanks in case Oliver had problems."

"Is that why you were following Ned?" Mike asked.

"Yes. I was upstairs in the food area when I saw Ned take something out of the tanks after the game. It seemed strange," Don Dixon said. "But I couldn't get down the stairs in time to stop him! I'm glad you two were here."

"Me too," Kate said. "Did you know Ned was stealing?"

"I had no idea," Don Dixon said. "A few weeks ago he asked me for a part-time job at my pet store, but I didn't need the help. Good thing I didn't hire him. He probably would have stolen some of *my* fish!"

Don Dixon took the covers off the coolers and looked at the baseball fish and turtles inside. "The police will need these, but I'll make sure they get back to your uncle," Don said. "He's the only person who's been able to breed baseball fish successfully. The Miami Marlins are special, but I think your uncle Oliver's favorite baseball fish, Marlin, is even more special."

Kate nodded in agreement. Then she glanced at the time. "Zikes! Come on, Mike," she said. "We're late. My mother's going to be looking for us!"

Late that night, Mike, Kate, Mrs. Hopkins, and Uncle Oliver were standing outside in the warm Miami air.

Out of nowhere, a piercing scream filled the night. Mike and Kate flinched. They turned around to try to find where the scream came from. But it was too dark.

"Are you sure this is safe?" Mrs. Hopkins asked.

Uncle Oliver laughed. "It's perfectly safe," he said. "I do this all the time."

A loud scream filled the night again.

"It sounds like a person," Kate said.

"It does. But it's not," Uncle Oliver said. "It's just a barn owl. They're found all over the United States, including in Florida. I love taking walks at night to hear the sounds of our animals!"

Uncle Oliver flipped on a big flashlight. They were standing on the wooden boardwalk at Panther Park.

"Come on, gang," he said. "Let me show you

something else." Uncle Oliver hadn't stopped smiling since Mike and Kate had told him how they had caught Ned with the stolen animals.

Earlier that evening, Ned had confessed at the police station. He admitted to catching endangered sea turtles and rare fish near Key Largo and putting them in the Marlins' tanks. He also admitted to stealing Uncle Oliver's baseball fish.

To sell the animals, Ned brought his customers to baseball games. They could see the stolen fish and turtles and bid on them. At the end of the games, Ned picked up the fish or turtles and brought them to the buyers. After he confessed, Ned gave the police the names of people who had bought the stolen animals. The police were working on getting the animals back.

The beam from Uncle Oliver's flashlight played on the wood of the walkway. "Ned was a great worker," Uncle Oliver said, shaking his head. "It's too bad he thought he could make money stealing turtles and selling my fish. I'm glad you two are so good at solving mysteries. It's good to have Marlin safe and sound back here at Panther Park!" He gave Mike and Kate high fives.

"But you said there wasn't enough money to keep Panther Park open. How will you take care of Marlin and the other animals?" Kate asked.

"That's the best part!" Uncle Oliver said. "Don Dixon called me a little while ago. He wants to invest in Panther Park. He thinks we can earn enough to keep going if he sells Panther Park tickets at his pet store!"

Mike pretended to swing a baseball bat. *"POW!"* he said. "That's what I call a home run!"

The path led straight to the panther area. Uncle Oliver flicked off the flashlight. It was pitch-black again. But Uncle Oliver seemed to know where to go. He led them a little farther through the dark. Then they stopped. Once their eyes got used to the dark, Mike and Kate started to make out the sights. Off in the distance, the barn owl screeched again.

The moon peeked out from behind the clouds. Its silvery light rippled across the clearing. As it did, Kate and Mike found themselves staring straight into the big yellow eyes of Uncle Oliver's panthers. Mike and Kate stood still until the animals started prowling from one side of their area to the other.

"I'm sure glad nobody tried to kidnap *them*!" Mike said.

"Shh . . . ," Uncle Oliver said. "I think I heard one of them say something!"

Mike and Kate listened. But all they heard was chirping and buzzing from the insects in the nearby bushes. In front of them, Uncle Oliver put a hand to his ear. He seemed to be listening to something that they couldn't hear.

Mike and Kate looked at each other. Mike pointed to his head and made circular motions with his finger like Uncle Oliver was cuckoo.

Then they heard it.

Prrrrrr. Prrrrrr.

The panthers were purring! They sounded almost like Kate's cat, Cooper, back home. Kate stepped closer to the animals to listen.

"*Now* you hear it," Uncle Oliver said. "But can you tell what they're saying?"

"No! Can you?" Kate asked.

"I think I can. It sounds to me like they're saying *thank you*," he said. "Thank you for finding the missing fish, saving the turtles, and rescuing the nature center and all the animals like us!"

Dugout Notes
☆ The Marlins' Ballpark ☆

Fish tanks. The Miami Marlins' stadium is unlike any other—it has two large fish tanks behind home plate! The tanks are built into the wall between the first row of seats and the infield. Each one is twenty-two feet long and holds 500 gallons of water.

Bobblehead Museum. Although Mike and Kate didn't visit it in the book, the Miami Marlins' stadium has a Bobblehead

Museum! Bobbleheads are small figures with big heads held on by springs. The springs allow the head to "bobble" back and forth. Miami's Bobblehead Museum is a single large display case. It holds close to 700 bobbleheads. The case even jiggles a little bit to keep the bobbleheads bobbling!

Marlins (the fish). A marlin is a type of large fish with a spearlike snout and a tall fin on its back. They can be up to fourteen feet long and weigh 1,800 pounds or more.

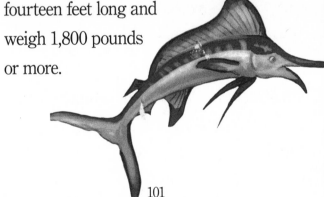

Marlins (the team). When it comes to baseball, the Miami Marlins are youngsters. The team started playing in 1993. Back then, they were called the Florida Marlins. When the Marlins moved to a new stadium in 2012, they changed their name to the Miami Marlins.

Florida panthers. Florida panthers are the state animal and an endangered species. They are usually tan with a white underbelly and black tips on their ears and tail. In other parts of the country, these large cats are known as cougars, mountain lions, or pumas. But in Florida they're called panthers.

Endangered turtles. There are a number of endangered turtles in Florida, including green sea turtles and hawksbill turtles. Baby green sea turtles are tiny, only about two inches long, but they can grow up to about four feet. They live around coral reefs, like the one where Kate and Mike went snorkeling.

Winners. Even though the Marlins are a young team, they've done better than some teams that have been around for a long time. The Marlins won the World Series in 1997 and in 2003!

Eephus pitch. There really is a trick pitch called the Eephus pitch. To throw an Eephus pitch, the pitcher tosses the ball high up in the air. The ball arcs up and drops down right over home plate. Only a few pitchers have ever used an Eephus pitch in a major-league game.

Junk balls. An Eephus pitch is a type of "junk" ball. Junk ball pitches are usually slow or move around a lot, so they're hard for batters to hit. Pitchers who throw lots of junk balls try to get the batters to "go fishing" and swing at bad pitches.

BATTER UP AND CRACK THE CASE!

BALLPARK ®
Mysteries

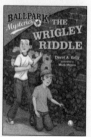

BASEBALL SLEUTHING FUN
WITH MORE TO COME!

RandomHouseKids.com